SEYMOUR and HENRY

Kim Lewis

WALKER BOOKS
AND SUBSIDIARIES
LONDON • BOSTON • SYDNEY • AUCKLAND

Seymour and Henry played in the pond.

PLOP went Seymour.

PLOP went Henry.

For my Flea

First published 2009 by Walker Books Ltd
87 Vauxhall Walk, London SE11 5HJ

2 4 6 8 10 9 7 5 3 1

© 2009 Kim Lewis

The right of Kim Lewis to be identified as author/illustrator of this
work has been asserted by her in accordance with the Copyright, Designs
and Patents Act 1988.

This book has been typeset in Malonia Voigo.

Printed in China

British Library Cataloguing in Publication Data: a catalogue record
for this book is available from the British Library

ISBN 978-1-4063-0610-1

www.walker.co.uk

All day long they swam
with Mummy.

Then Mummy flapped her wings.
"Come along, my little ducks,"
she said. "It's time
we all went home."

But the ducklings kept on playing.

They didn't want to stop.

"Quack!" said Seymour.

"Quack!" said Henry.

They ran away from Mummy.

Pit-a-pat went Seymour.

Pit-a-pat went Henry.

Seymour hopped
up on a log.

Henry wriggled
under.

Seymour hurried
round a rock.

Round and round
ran Henry.

The ducklings ran a little further.

Pit-a-pat they scampered –

through tall grass

and down a slope.

Slippy-slidey-bump,
they landed.

Then the little
ducklings hid.

"Quack!"
giggled Seymour.
"Quack!"
giggled Henry.

They waited
for Mummy
to come and
find them.

They waited.

And waited.

PLIP, PLOP came
some drops of rain.
They fell on
Seymour's head.

PLIP, PLOP
more drops came.
They fell on
Henry too.

PLIP-PLOP, PLIP-PLOP the rain fell down.

"QUACK!" the ducklings cried.

Pit-a-pat went Seymour.

Pit-a-pat went Henry.

up the slope
and through
the grass,

round
the rock

and under

the log,

they ran as fast as they could go.

And there was Mummy, waiting for them.

"Quack!" said Seymour.

"Quack!" said Henry.

PLIP-PLOP, PLIP-PLOP went the rain.

The little ducklings skipped

and danced.

Then Mummy flapped her wings.

"Come along, my little ducks," she said.

"Hop on for a ride."

"Quack!" sang Seymour.

"Quack!" sang Henry.

And pit-a-pat, pit-a-pat

Mummy took her ducklings . . .

. . . home.